The SPORTS HEROES Library

Track's
MAGNIFICENT
MILERS

Nathan Aaseng

Lerner Publications Company • Minneapolis

Cover photograph: Steve Ovett (279) prepares to unleash the final sprint that had earned him 42 straight victories before this 1,500-meter race at the 1980 Moscow Olympics. Coe (254), his chief rival, knows that Ovett is on his shoulder.

ACKNOWLEDGMENTS: The photographs are reproduced through the courtesy of: pp. 4, 7, 8, 17, 25, 30, 33, 37, 46, 49, 51, 57, 59, 61, 62, 68, 74, 77, 79, Wide World Photos, Inc.; p. 10, University of Kansas; p. 39, Kansas State Historical Society, Topeka.
Cover photograph © All Sport/Don Morley

*To Murray, Jacobsen, Williamson, Damerval,
Potter, and all those guys*

LIBRARY OF CONGRESS CATALOGING IN PUBLICATION DATA

Aaseng, Nathan.
  Track's magnificent milers.

  (The Sports heroes library)
  SUMMARY: Biographies of world record-breaking mile runners, including Glenn Cunningham, Roger Bannister, Herb Elliott, Jim Ryun, Kip Keino, John Walker, Filbert Bayi, Sebastian Coe, and Mary Decker.

  1. Runners (Sports)—Biography—Juvenile literature.
[1. Runners (Sports) 2. Track and field athletes] I. Title.

GV697.A1A22   796.4'26 [B] [920]   80-27404
ISBN 0-8225-1066-9   AACRI

Manufactured in the United States of America.

International Standard Book Number: 0-8225-1066-9
Library of Congress Catalog Card Number: 80-27404

1 2 3 4 5 6 7 8 9 10 90 89 88 87 86 85 84 83 82 81

Contents

Britain's Roger Bannister shows the strain of running the world's first *sub*-four-minute mile on May 6, 1954.

Introduction

The mile run has always been the glamour event of track and field, and no other event has had such an exciting history. The mile has seen some of the most heroic efforts and desperate person-to-person duels in the history of sports. And attempts to break the four-minute mile have certainly provided some of sports' most thrilling moments.

What makes the mile so special? One reason is because, in many ways, the mile is the perfect race. No other running event requires quite the combination of endurance, speed, ingenuity and strength that the mile does. As examples of endurance, mile fans are amazed at the tireless stride of Mary Decker, and they will never forget the grueling pace of Glenn Cunningham. The blazing kick of Jim Ryun was as exciting a demonstration of raw speed as any sprint race. Roger Bannister's ability to win a mile race on clever strategy, and John Walker's use of strength to pull ahead at the end of a close race drew thousands of spectators to the track.

Another reason for the popularity of the mile is that it is one of the easiest races to watch. Sprints are over too quickly, and distance races do not have the same tension as the mile until the final laps. But the mile can hold spectators on the edges of their seats for four tension-packed minutes because great milers can make their moves during any second of the race.

In the Olympics, some of track's most exciting moments have happened as the world's best milers made their final sprints for the gold medal. Fans were holding their breath when miler Herb Elliott in 1960 and Filbert Bayi in the 1974 Olympics set new world records. But in the Olympics, it's not mile records that milers set out to break. Because all of the Olympic events are run in meters, milers compete in the 1,500-meter run, about 100 yards short of a mile.

While some running events like the mile have not changed through the years, running itself has

Mary Decker, the United States' top woman distance runner, breaks the tape at 4:00.87 and sets another U.S. 1,500-meter record.

High school sensation Jim Ryun relaxes after qualifying for the 1964 U.S. Olymic team in the 1,500-meter race.

changed. Today running has become a science, and races are now run on tracks made of rubbery, artificial material to make it comfortable for runners in all kinds of weather. And training for runners has changed, too. Runners today battle through exhausting workouts while coaches, and even scientists, observe their progress. Newspapers, magazines, and books are filled with information to help runners learn everything about the sport from what foods to eat to what shoes to wear. Even at grade school meets, tracks are filled with people holding clipboards and wearing stopwatches around their necks.

But in spite of today's changes in the sport of running, the famous mile runners in this book are much like the racers of long ago. Their love of running is the most important part of success, just as it has always been. They know a race is as much a battle against themselves as it is against their opponents. The ten runners in this book—most who have enjoyed running since they were very young—have all risen to the challenge of the mile run. They have forced themselves to go faster than any other man or woman before them.

Few runners ever saw this view of Glenn Cunningham during a race. In most races, they only saw his back!

10

1
Glenn Cunningham

On a cold morning in 1916, 7-year-old Glenn Cunningham and his older brother Floyd left their Kansas farm and trotted to school. Since the Cunningham boys were usually the first to arrive at the country schoolhouse, it was their job to start the fire in the coal stove to warm up the building. That morning, just as they had done many times before, the boys picked up the fuel can and poured over the coals what they thought was kerosene. But someone had made a deadly mistake. Instead of kerosene, the can had been filled with gasoline.

When the match touched the gasoline, the building quickly exploded into flames. The boys were instantly thrown back and surrounded by fire. Even though his legs were on fire, Glenn managed to find his way out of the building. Once outside, he rolled around in the snow to put out the flames burning his body. When Floyd finally staggered out of the schoolhouse, he was burned even worse than Glenn. Both boys were in incredible pain, but they managed to get all the way back to their home before they collapsed.

The doctors were unable to save Floyd's life, and at first they thought Glenn might not make it either. After they were sure he was going to live, the doctors gave Glenn the bad news: his legs had been so badly damaged that he would probably never walk again. Glenn refused to believe this, and he stubbornly told the doctors he would not only walk again—he would also run. To the doctors this seemed impossible because the fire had completely destroyed the arch in one of Glenn's feet.

But Glenn was determined and would not give up on his goal of walking again. As soon as the scars on his legs had toughened, he began an exercise program. His mother would rub and bend his stiff legs for hours at a time. When his mother became tired, Glenn would take over. All of this exercising was terribly painful, but Glenn was determined to get back on his feet.

After many months of work, Glenn could finally stand by himself. And one day when the doctor came by for a visit, he was shocked to see young Cunningham walking.

It took several years for Glenn to walk without a limp, and by then he had started to run. For Glenn running was a joy, and he never forgot how lucky he was to be able to use his legs again. He worked so hard at running that his legs became even stronger than those of most boys.

One day Glenn just happened to see a display of medals in a store window in his home town of Elkhart, Kansas. The medals were to be awarded at a local high school track meet that afternoon. Glenn was so impressed by the medals that right then he decided to enter his first real race. Although he was supposed to go home right after school, Glenn stayed for the race. He ran the mile and won.

Winning this race was a special triumph for Glenn. By winning, Glenn—who at one time was never expected to walk again—had shown how far a person could go with determination. After that race, Glenn promised himself that he would someday help others to overcome their problems.

Glenn went on to win his share of races during high school, but he did not gain much attention.

In fact, at that time no American miler had ever become famous. But Glenn received enough encouragement to enroll at the University of Kansas and continue running.

When Glenn was in college in the late 1920s, the Great Depression was hitting the country. Money was hard to come by, and Glenn had to work full time to pay for his education. But Glenn not only managed to earn enough to pay for his school expenses, he was also able to loan money to farmers he knew who were also hit hard by the depression. Between working and studying, it was a wonder that Glenn found the time to run track.

In addition to his financial problems and his damaged legs, Glenn faced another handicap in his drive to become a winning runner. At 5 feet, 9 inches, and a stocky 165 pounds, Glenn's body seemed built more for lifting weights than for running the mile. Because of his size, Glenn didn't have the fast sprinting speed of other milers. But he continued to push himself to get the most out of the endurance that he had. In most of his meets for the University of Kansas, Glenn ran both the mile and the half-mile in the same day.

Glenn's hours of practice paid off in 1932 when he ran a mile in 4 minutes, 14.3 seconds (4:14.3), one of the fastest ever run in the United States. He soon followed that time with an American record of 4:11.1.

Now the track world took notice, and the story of Glenn Cunningham's accident and determination was repeated throughout the country. Wherever he ran, thousands of fans came to watch this new track star in action. They followed his progress, hoping he would win a gold medal in the 1,500-meter race in the 1932 Olympics. But in the Games held in Los Angeles, Glenn had to settle for fourth place because he lacked finishing speed. When he took a trip to Europe the following summer, however, he once again thrilled his fans. The stocky runner entered 20 races and won them all!

Cunningham's style of racing soon earned him the nickname "Kansas Ironman." Because he did not have the finishing speed of some of his rivals, Glenn had to depend on his superior endurance to run them into the ground. Glenn liked to charge into the lead at the halfway point and then try to keep a grueling pace until the end. This half-mile burst became a Cunningham trademark. Opponents dreaded the Kansas Ironman's long surge to the finishing tape.

Glenn's biggest triumph came in 1934 when he

broke the world record for the mile. Running on a track in Princeton, New Jersey, he covered the distance in 4:06.8. That same year, he topped the world indoor record for 1,500 meters at 3:52.2 but lost the race by only a step.

In the 1936 Olympics, Cunningham again led during most of the 1,500-meter race. But an Italian runner outsprinted him to the finish, and Glenn had to settle for the silver medal. Cunningham knew he would continue to lose unless he began forcing the pace earlier and earlier in the race.

By the middle of the 1930s, most of Glenn's rivals had dropped out of the sport. But Glenn stayed with running and ran harder than ever. The familiar scarred legs carried him to five national championships in the 1,500 meter—in 1933 (3:52.3), 1935 (3:52.1), 1936 (3:54.2), 1937 (3:51.8), and 1938 (3:52.5).

In 1938 Glenn set out to run his best time ever. In order to run the fastest possible pace, Glenn had other runners start out ahead of him at different times. Then he took off, catching up to them one by one. When he finished, his time of 4:04.4 had again topped the old world record. But because of the unusual method of giving the other runners a head start, the record was not allowed.

Cunningham outlasted the strong sprints of his rivals to capture his fourth national 1,500-meter title in 1937. His time was 3:51.8.

After a long career, Glenn decided to call it quits in 1940. His last race in Fresno, California, was a true Cunningham effort. Glenn beat the fastest time ever run for 1,500 meters—3:47.0. Though he was again nosed out at the finish line, he lost by only one second and forced the winner to run a world record to beat him!

Thoughout his career and in his retirement, Glenn never forgot his promise to help others. After earning his Master's and PhD degrees at New York University, he bought a large ranch in Kansas. Over the years, the Cunningham ranch became home for many troubled kids, and more than 8,000 children were helped by Glenn. No matter how much of a problem they were, Glenn never turned any children away. The world's first famous miler knew that even the most serious of difficulties could usually be overcome with determination.

2
Roger
Bannister

Training for a world record in the mile run is a full-time job. In one year, top runners often cover as many miles on foot as most people travel in cars. But one of the most famous milers in history treated running as a hobby. The only time Roger Bannister spent running was during his lunch hour. And he never ran seven days a week in his life. Yet Roger became the first human to break the magic four-minute barrier in the mile.

Roger Gilbert Bannister was born in Harlow, England, in 1929. As a young boy, Roger ran almost everywhere he went and said it was much easier than walking. But like Glenn Cunningham, Roger had nothing to do with track until he was in high school. And, although he ran in high school, it was not until 1946, when he was 17 years old and out of school, that Bannister first raced around a track.

When Roger realized he had some skill in competitive running, he became his own coach and began to experiment with training methods and schedules. In the beginning, training for Roger consisted of only one workout and one race per week. This wasn't because Roger was lazy but because he had other interests besides running. Most of all, Roger wanted to become a doctor, and he didn't want anything to get in the way of that goal. By the time he entered Oxford University in 1946 at the age of 17, Roger had increased his workouts to three or four per week. But he still kept his runs to only one half hour.

Bannister's training methods seemed to be working, and by 1950 his running times began to attract notice. But the more attention Roger received, the more track experts scoffed at his training methods. How could he hope to compete with top runners when he spent so little time training, they commented. The final straw came when Bannister stated he could only do six pushups. Then experts were convinced that Roger didn't know anything about getting himself in shape.

But Roger didn't see why he should change. With

all of the time he spent studying, he didn't have time to lift weights or to do all of the exercises the other runners did. So he figured the best way to become a good runner was simply to run.

In 1951 Roger found the perfect way to silence his critics. He beat everybody in his races! His time of 4:07.8 in one race that year showed that he really could get into shape with just his noontime runs. As his times for the mile continued to hover just over four minutes, Bannister became the favorite to win the 1,500-meter race at the 1952 Olympics.

But not even preparing for the Olympics could sway Roger from his studies. If anything, he put in even less running time than usual during the winter before the Olympics. In fact, Bannister did not even race in 1952 until late May. He figured it wouldn't take long to prepare for one Olympic race.

But Roger had a surprise in store for him at the Helsinki Olympics. Because there were so many entries in the 1,500-meter race, officials decided to run the event with trial heats. The track, then, would not be so crowded for the finals. Roger was stunned. He knew he could handle one race, but now he would have to run hard just to make the finals.

In his trial heat to gain the finals, Roger ran through the pack of runners, as expected. But as the gun went off in the final race, Roger discovered he was tired and weak. After struggling through the entire race, Roger finished fourth.

After the Olympics, Bannister was ready to give up running. But fortunately the attack on the "Four-Minute Mile" by the world's fastest runners caught his attention. Some people claimed no one could run a mile under four minutes, and the world's top runners were trying to prove them wrong. In 1953 John Landy of Australia had made several all-out efforts to break the four-minute time, but he had always come up about two seconds slow.

It had been almost 100 years since the five-minute mile had been broken in Dublin. Now it seemed it was just a matter of time before someone broke the four-minute mile. And Roger wanted to be the first to do it.

In order to prepare for his attack on the four-minute mile, Roger stepped up his practices to five a week. (But he still kept his noon runs to 45 minutes or less.) By the beginning of May 1954, after a five-day rest, Roger was ready to try.

On race day, May 6, it looked like the cold,

windy weather would make it impossible for Bannister to run a record race. Glumly, Roger called his parents and told them not to come. But they showed up anyway and joined the small crowd of spectators at the Iffley Road track at Oxford. By race time, the wind had died down. Maybe this will be the day, the crowd thought.

Roger's Oxford teammates took turns pacing him in the run. They covered the first half mile in 1:58. It was a fast pace, but John Landy had started just as quickly in his attempts to break the four-minute mile. The pace felt easy to Bannister, and he breezed through the third lap. But as he was running the fourth lap, the strain caught up with him, and he began to feel as though he were running in a suit of heavy armor. With each step every muscle grew heavier. As Bannister rounded the final turn he was in agony, and the finish line seemed impossibly far away. But in spite of the pain, Bannister drove his 6-foot, 2-inch, 154-pound body to the finish and collapsed.

The timers eagerly looked at their watches. "Three—" was all the crowd needed to hear. They broke into cheers for the first sub-four-minute mile. Bannister's 3:59.4 had just made him the most famous athlete in the world.

On June 21 in Finland, only weeks after Bannister's landmark race, John Landy of Australia ran the mile at 3:57.9 to break Bannister's record and set the stage for a historic rematch. This would be the final race of Roger's career. Called the "Mile of the Century," it would be run in Vancouver, Canada, between the two men who had broken the four-minute mark.

August 7 was the day of the Bannister-Landy contest. When the starting gun shot off, Landy sped off to a lead. At the half-mile mark, he had increased his lead to 10 yards. Bannister's strategy had been to stay relaxed until the final quarter. But now he had to press on or Landy's lead would be too large to overcome.

Fighting off pain and exhaustion, Roger pulled up behind Landy, hoping his rival would tire. Then Roger decided it was time to make one final effort to pass Landy.

The crowd was shouting wildly. Even though he was right on Landy's heels, Landy could not hear Bannister because there was so much noise. Just as Landy turned to see where his opponent was, Bannister blew past him. Landy never recovered from the surprise, and Roger won the race in his best time ever—3:58.8.

In the "Mile of the Century," Australia's John Landy (300) never recovered from Roger Bannister's sudden burst of speed. Bannister won the race in his best time of 3:58.8. Landy was less than one second behind at 3:59.6.

After his race with Landy, Bannister would have liked to try for the gold medal in the 1956 Olympic Games in Melbourne, Australia, but his studies again won out over running. Bannister retired from racing at the age of 25 and went on to become a highly respected medical doctor in London.

Since that May race in 1954, hundreds of men have beaten Bannister's famous time of 3:59.4. But Roger was the first man to break the four-minute mile, and that achievement is considered one of the highlights in the world of sports.

3
Herb
Elliott

It's too bad that Herb Elliot was running 10 years before the back-to-nature movement became popular. Makers of wheat germ and other foods would have loved to use Herb in their commercials. Herb believed that raw, natural foods were the only foods a serious runner should eat. And his running successes certainly seem to be a strong argument for such a diet, because Elliott was perhaps the greatest miler of all time. Even though others have beaten his best mile, the fact remains that Herb *never* lost a single mile race to anyone!

Elliott was born in 1938 in Perth, Australia, and he began running at an early age. The sandy beaches and rugged hills around his hometown made running a stiff challenge. But young Herb enjoyed a good test of his abilities. By the time he was 14, Herb was determined to become a serious runner and was running the mile in 5:35. After another year of workouts on Perth's challenging terrain, Elliott had dropped his best mile time to 4:21. This was quite an achievement for a 15 year old.

In 1955, when he was 17 years old, Elliott's promising career was nearly ruined by an accident. Herb broke his foot while helping to move a heavy piano. After weeks of sitting around in a cast, Herb lost interest in running. But fortunately the 1956 Olympic Games were held in Australia. After seeing the 1,500-meter race in person, Herb could not wait to go out and win races himself.

With his old determination, Elliott began racing again, and he soon proved good enough to be invited to the training camp of Coach Percy Cerutty in Port Sea, Victoria. Cerutty's ideas on how to train were different from those of most coaches. Cerutty did not believe in using a stopwatch to time practices. Instead he let his athletes run just as hard as they wanted to. The best athletes, Cerutty reasoned, would take pride in pushing themselves to the point of exhaustion. Cerutty also believed in eating natural foods and in lifting weights to build a strong body for running.

By following Cerutty's advice, Elliott developed into one of the strongest men to run the mile. Those who visited Cerutty's training camp could hardly believe the punishment Elliott would endure on a run. The few foolish ones who tried to run with him in a workout were left gasping for air. Elliott's incredible speed through deep sand and his furious burst through woods discouraged even the toughest of runners from keeping up with him.

Herb's strenuous program paid off right away and in 1958, at the age of 19, he was running the mile at better than 4:05. Elliott had the top veteran runners worried. They figured if anyone was going to beat the youngster, it would be while he was still inexperienced. But during 1958, Herb ran against the best and won every time. Some thought he was just lucky. They were sure he would be taught a lesson in Dublin, Ireland, later that year.

Nearly all of the best milers in Herb's day were in Dublin on August 6 for that race. Spurred on by the excitement and the fierce competition, the pack of runners toured the first half mile in a brisk 1:58. Despite the fast pace, Elliott felt as fresh as if he were just warming up. So when a determined Mervyn Lincoln, a fellow Australian, shot into the lead on the third lap, Herb went with him. Lincoln

In this 1958 Dublin race, the four trailing runners all bettered the four-minute mile. But their times weren't fast enough to catch front-runner, Herb Elliott, who had a record-shattering time of 3:54.5.

could not pull away from his young rival, and soon Elliott roared to the front. Opening up a wide lead, Herb poured it on all the way to the finish line. His time of 3:54.5 made his rivals despair. The young Australian had beaten the world record by nearly *three* seconds!

A few days after the Dublin mile race, Elliott approached the starting line for a 1,500-meter race in Goteborg, Sweden. A friend joked with Elliott and bet him a bottle of vodka that he wouldn't break another world's record. But any bet against Herb was a foolish one. Herb's time of 3:36 in that race was 2.1 seconds faster than the old world record set the previous year.

By 1959 Elliott was winning so easily that he took the fight out of most milers. That year there were few fine mile efforts by anyone. Elliott himself seemed to be losing interest in the sport again, and he took a break from the usual punishment of training. It was during this break that Elliott did the worst thing a distance runner could do for his lungs. He started smoking.

Because of his heavy smoking, Elliott was in poor physical condition when he again raced against Mervyn Lincoln, one of his few remaining competitors, in Brisbane, Australia, on March 14, 1959. For most of the race, Elliott hung close to Lincoln. Lincoln was leading, and he was convinced it would be just a matter of time before Elliott's poor health would cause him to slow down. But on the final lap, Herb suddenly flew past Mervyn and sprinted for the finish line in a time of 3:58.9. The startled Lincoln did not even come close. Even when he was out of shape, Elliott had proven to be unbeatable.

But Herb had learned a lesson from his race with Lincoln. No run had ever hurt him as badly as that one had, and it was a long time before he fully recovered from the pain. From then on, Herb decided running was serious business. So as the time for the 1960 Olympics approached, Herb began a rigorous program.

In the 1960 games in Rome, Elliott easily made it into the finals of the 1,500-meter race. But the qualifying runs had left him feeling strangely tired. When the starting gun went off for the finals, Elliott stayed near the middle of the pack, watching his opponents warily. Even the first two laps were a struggle for him. His body didn't seem to be running smoothly, and his legs had little spring.

As the runners moved well into the third lap, Elliott knew he would have to make his move if he wanted to win. Suddenly he sprinted by everyone and ran as if his life were in danger. His lead widened, but he was still worried.

Suddenly Herb saw his coach on the track's in-field, waving his towel wildly. That was the signal that Herb was on his way to a very fast time! Herb ran the entire last lap with all his might and won easily. It was another world record for Herb, and his time of 3:35.6 had broken his previous record.

Elliott (center) stands tall on the victory platform after winning the gold medal in the 1,500 meter at the 1960 Olympics. Runners from Hungary (left) and France (right) placed third and second.

Following his Olympic win, Elliot ran a schedule that would have worn down the mechanical rabbit at a dog track. He raced 11 times in just 19 days and won all of the mile events. Though he raced well, the long grind finally took the desire to run out of him, and he gave up his track career at the age of 22. From start to finish, his racing career had lasted only six years.

But Herb Elliott had trained and raced with enough fury to last for a lifetime. Even when he was sick, tired, or out of shape, he always showed he had enough to win. When he retired, Elliott had run the two fastest mile races of all time—3:54.5 and 3:55.4—and the three fastest 1,500-meter races —3:36.0, 3:37.4, and 3:35.6. If he would have kept up his training for just a few more years, there is no telling by how much time the unbeatable Herb Elliott could have lowered the mile record.

4
Jim
Ryun

In a mile race in 1964, Jim Ryun placed eighth with a time of 3:59.0. Yet even the winner of the race went out of his way to congratulate Jim, an unknown runner, on the fine race he had run. Four years later, Ryun placed second in a much more important meet—the 1968 Olympics in Mexico City. In that race, Ryun nearly broke the old Olympic record for the 1,500-meter run. But he was called a failure.

As Jim learned from these two races, praise is not always based on where a runner finishes, or even on how hard he or she tries. Before the first race, Jim had been an unknown high school kid. At the time of the second race, he was the best miler in the world. From a runner as good as Ryun, people expected more than just a good effort.

Ryun was such a fine runner that the fans at the Olympics were shocked to find out he could actually lose a race.

Jim was born in Wichita, Kansas, in 1947. From an early age, he always wanted to do well in sports. But as he was growing up, it seemed as though the tall, gangly Ryun would never have enough coordination to be a star athlete. Besides he was often sick and had ear problems.

Unlike most of the great milers, running did not come naturally for Jim. Jim tried running the 440-yard dash in junior high school, but he wasn't fast enough to win a spot on the team. And when he tried to race cross-country, the workouts were too hard for him to finish. In the autumn of 1963 when he was 15, Ryun came home from his first mile race—a 5:38 mile—too sick to eat his dinner.

That same autumn, one of the most mysterious events in the history of sports happened to Jim. One day he was only good enough to run on the "B" squad at his high school. But one month later, he suddenly finished sixth in the Kansas state high school meet. Ryun's coach must have wondered if he were dreaming when he saw Jim running so fast!

But Jim's sudden success was real. The following spring, he beat the defending state champion miler

Although he did not win this race, Kansas schoolboy Jim Ryun (right) stunned the track world by keeping pace with North America's top milers. Dyrol Burleson (34) came in first.

with a time of 4:26.4. After that, Ryun ran each race faster than the one before. In a race against a college runner, Ryun ran an amazing 4:08 mile.

While still in high school, Ryun accepted an invitation to go to California to take on the best runners in the United States. As he walked to the starting lane, Ryun was thrilled to be racing against such well-known, top-rated runners as Tom O'Hara and Dyrol Burleson. During the race, the high schooler managed to keep up with the blazing pace set by the older men. Though Ryun did not finish near the leaders, with a time of 3:59.0 he became the first high school student to break four minutes in the mile. This was an incredible performance since Jim had only recently started running. Everyone agreed that one day Ryun would be one of the best milers in the world.

In the trial for the 1964 United States' Olympics team, Jim battled veteran runners, hoping to be one of the three who would earn a spot in the Olympics that year. O'Hara and Burleson were still out of Ryun's class in the 1,500-meter run, but Ryun felt he had a chance to win the third spot.

At the Olympic tryouts, a tough, experienced trackman named Jim Grelle wanted third place as much as Ryun did. Near the end of the race, Ryun and Grelle battled side by side down the final straightaway. As they approached the finish line, Grelle made a desperate dive, but Ryun just nosed him out to earn the third spot on the team. As it turned out, Ryun almost wished that Grelle had beaten him. In the Games, Jim came down with the flu and finished last in his 1,500-meter heat.

After his disappointment at the Tokyo Olympics, Jim continued running at the University of Kansas,

At the 1965 National AAU meet in San Diego, Ryun's deadly finishing kick claims more victims.

Glenn Cunningham's old school. It was here that Ryun achieved most of his fame. The lean, 6-foot, 1-inch Ryun quickly became a favorite of college track fans. In the final lap of a race, even fans who knew little about track expected to see Ryun's shocking red-and-blue uniform blaze into the lead.

As Jim's career progressed, he proved to be one of the first milers with a true sprinter's speed. In

39

fact, his first world record actually came in an 880-yard race when he ran a blistering time of 1:44.9 seconds in 1966.

Fewer than 1,000 fans had been on hand to see Ryun set his first world record. But when Jim traveled to Berkeley, California, later that summer to try for his second world record, 15,000 fans crowded the stands to see him.

That day, July 17, seemed ideal for a good race. The weather was so comfortable that Jim nearly fell asleep while relaxing before the race. The only thing Jim needed to help him push himself to his best performance was a fast rival. As the race began, a runner named Wade Bell gave Ryun all the push he needed. After leading the pack of runners at a dangerously fast time of 1:55.5 for the first half-mile, Bell continued to run at the same pace.

Toward the end of the race, Ryun took over, but the crowd did not get to see the famous Ryun finish. The pace had been far too fast for a final sprint, and Ryun had to struggle just to keep up the same speed. With his legs pumping furiously, Ryun crossed the finish line with a time of 3:51.3. He had just shattered the world's mile record, previously held by Michel Jazy of France, by 2.3 seconds!

During the next year, 1967, Ryun continued to rule the middle-distance events (the mile, half-mile, 800 meter and 1,500 meter), and he ran his best race ever. Ryun started out very slowly in this race, but he gradually lengthened his stride and began to move faster. Going into the final quarter-mile, Ryun exploded as if running only a short sprint. The entire last lap was unlike anything anyone had ever seen in a mile race before. Jim sped around to the finish line with frightening speed. Despite his slow start, he had beat his own world record with a time of 3:51.1!

Now all that remained for Ryun was to win a gold medal in the Olympics. But as he prepared for the 1968 Games, the breaks seemed to be going against him. Early in the year, Ryun became ill with mononucleosis. Even though he recovered more quickly than expected, the illness weakened him and threw him off his training schedule.

Worse yet, the 1968 Olympics were being held in Mexico City at an altitude of 7,600 feet. Kip Keino from Kenya, Ryun's main rival in the 1,500 meter, was used to running in the mountains where the air was thin. This would give Keino a big advantage over Ryun. Jim knew he could not hope to get his body used to such running conditions in the short amount of time he had.

In the finals at the Olympics, Keino ran a fast, steady pace, and Ryun could not keep up. Though Ryun closed the gap on the final lap, he finished second at 3:37.8 to Keino's time of 3:34.9. American track fans were shocked. They had expected Jim's strong finish to win as it had always done before. They called Ryun a flop. After that, running was not much fun for Jim, and he quit the following year.

But in 1970 Jim started a gallant comeback effort to win the gold medal he had lost. He fought off allergies and top runners like Marty Liquori to become the best miler in the United States. After a fine effort in running a 3:52.8 mile and later a victory in the 1972 Olympic trials, Jim seemed ready. Ryun's old rival, Keino, was also entered in the 1,500 meter. It seemed that Jim would now have his chance to get even—and this time at sea level.

In his trial heat for the Olympics, Ryun ran among a large cluster of runners. With about 500 yards to go, Jim decided he had better make his move. So he started to pass runners on the turn. As he moved through the middle of the pack, he and another runner, Billy Fordjour from Ghana, suddenly fell. Ryun lay on the ground in shock, his ankles, knees, and one of his hips throbbing from the pain of the fall. Ryun got up, hobbled a few steps, and broke into a sprint. But it was too late to even try to qualify.

Ryun's coaches asked the judges to give Jim another chance. After all, they said, he had been tripped by another runner. But Jim did not get another chance.

Even sports experts sometimes forget that any athlete needs one very important thing in order to be a winner—luck. Ryun had had none. But even with his misfortunes, Jim had proved to be one of the greatest milers of his time. His world record for the mile stood for 8 years before it was topped. And his American record for the mile has stood for over 12 years.

5
Kip
Keino

Hezekiah Kipchoge Keino was born in Kenya in 1940, the year Glenn Cunningham retired. But few people in Kenya had ever heard of Glenn Cunningham, the Kansas Ironman. Though it was popular, racing was a completely different sport in Kenya. When young Kip began racing there were no coaches, stopwatches, or even tracks. Instead of a medal or a trophy, Kip won a bar of soap for his first victory.

Even though Kip's father had been a fine distance runner, he didn't give his son any formal workout. Most of Kip's running was done in the hills where he spent his time herding goats. Life was a struggle for Kip, and he had little time to think about training to be a runner. Kip even had to struggle to be able to go to school. When he was eleven, he sneaked off to attend a school. But since he had no money, he was forced to return home and was beaten by his father for running away.

In his late teens, Keino joined the Kenyan police force and was assigned to his home district. He still knew nothing about distance training, but his job kept him in top physical condition. By now Kip was entering and winning races around the country, and he even won a national championship race. Kip was proving to be a tireless runner who could run an endless number of races. By 1963 Kip's running ability had earned him a job as a physical education instructor on the police force.

The following year, Kip represented his country in the 1964 Olympics in Tokyo. Among the world's top runners, Kip went largely unnoticed. African runners were just starting to gain attention from other parts of the world. Most track experts knew little about any African distance runners other than Abebe Bikila, the man who had won the 1960 Olympic marathon. In the 1964 Games, Kip failed to earn a spot in the finals of the 1,500 meter. But he placed fifth in the finals of the 5,000-meter (about 3 miles) race.

Kip's experience in Tokyo made him eager to learn more about racing. A former United States

After saving their strength for most of the 1,500 race, Olympic runners battled furiously to qualify for the finals. Keino (right) placed fifth in the semi-finals and was barely edged out in his bid.

trackman, Mel Whitfield, had talked to Kip about the importance of training and had given him a sample workout schedule. Though Kip still had no coach—and never did—he followed Whitfield's schedule so he could learn how to train better.

Keino became an especially strong runner because of "resistance" training. Resistance training is like a baseball player swinging an extra-heavy bat before he faces a pitcher. After swinging the heavy bat, the regular one is easier to swing. While training, Kip tried running in army boots so his legs would feel lighter when he ran without them in a race. And because Kip ran most of his life in the thin air of high altitudes where the air was richer, running became especially easy for Kip.

In spite of his new knowledge about training, Kip still had some unusual running habits. When he ran, Keino liked to wear a bright orange cap. At the start of his final kick, he would fling the cap into the infield!

Some of Keino's running strategies seemed as unusual as his cap-throwing trademark. For example, experts could not understand why he was running mile races. Keino seemed better suited to longer races. After all, it took either a sense of pace or a fast-finishing kick to make a good miler. And Kip was slower than most milers. He had little sense of pace and had no idea what lap times were all about. When he ran, there was no telling during which lap Kip would feel like running fast and in which lap he would slow down.

But Keino was tireless, and he had a strategy all his own. He knew he could start out quickly and still have enough strength to finish the race.

His 5-foot, 9-inch, 145-pound body ran so smoothly that he never seemed to be working at running.

In 1966 Kip ran a mile time of 3:54.2, which made him the top threat to America's Jim Ryun. Though Ryun beat Keino badly in a Los Angeles race in 1967, track experts were wary of Keino. After all, the 1968 Olympics would be held in Mexico City at an altitude of 7,600 feet, and Keino was more used to running at that elevation than Ryun was.

When Olympic officials saw Kip's plans for the 1968 Olympics, they could hardly believe them. Instead of saving himself for a match with Ryun in the 1,500-meter race, Kip planned to run the 5,000- and the 10,000-meter races as well! That meant hard qualifying races in both the 1,500 and 5,000, as well as in the three final races.

As the trial heats began Kip refused to save his strength, and he set an exhausting pace in every run he made. Even when he could have slowed down and still qualify for the finals, Keino pressed on and showed no signs of ever getting tired. He came within two-tenths of a second of winning the 5,000-meter race with a time of 14:05.2.

Although Keino's legs never showed any signs of strain, his stomach did. Kip had such pains after his first races that doctors told him to stop running. But the sleek runner was not through with the Olympics. The final match—the 1,500 meter— with Jim Ryun awaited.

Kip decided there was only one way to beat the speedier Ryun. He would make Ryun run so fast that he would be too worn out to sprint at the end. Fellow Kenyan Ben Jipcho gave Kip some help. Jipcho led the first part of the race at a

Keino opens up a huge lead in the mile-high Olympics at Mexico City while, 15 yards behind, Ryun gasps in the thin air.

grueling pace while Kip stayed in the rear. Jipcho's fast running exhausted most of the other runners as he blazed the first half mile in 1:55. Then Kip took off and kept pushing the pace.

Far back in the pack, Ryun waited for Keino to fade. After the number of tough races Kip had run, most people expected the Kenyan would be lucky to finish at all at that pace. But Kip glided along, comfortable as ever, as Ryun made a desperate drive to catch him. While the high altitude was an advantage for Keino, it robbed Ryun of the air he needed to unleash his powerful sprint. Keino won the race in a record time of 3:34.9.

Four years later, in 1972, Keino returned to the Olympics in Munich, West Germany. Even though he was older and wiser, Kip still refused to settle for one race. First he ran the 1,500 and, in an extremely close contest, finished in 3:36.8, only 5/10ths of a second behind the winner, Pekka Vasala from Finland. Then, he tried the steeplechase (a 3,000-meter race with hurdles and a water jump). Despite his poor hurdling form, Keino had enough raw strength to come in first, taking home another gold medal.

After his tremendous success, Keino was promoted to a high rank in the Kenyan police force.

Although he showed the awkward form of a beginner at the hurdles, Keino still won the gold medal in the 1972 Olympic 3,000-meter steeplechase. Also jumping the barrier is Keino's teammate, Ben Jipcho (574). Jipcho had helped Keino to beat Ryun in the 1,500 meter at the 1968 Olympics.

But more important than his new job was the way he promoted other African distance runners. Keino's exciting style led the way for such great runners as Ben Jipcho, Mike Boit, and Filbert Bayi to challenge the world. Keino had showed them that they—just like he—could overcome a lack of training and coaching to beat the best runners in the world.

6
John Walker
& Filbert Bayi

In the world of track, it is difficult to imagine two more unusual runners than John Walker of New Zealand and Filbert Bayi of Tanzania. Walker was not *built* like the usual miler, and Bayi did not *race* like the usual miler. How either one of them could have become a world-class runner was a mystery to experienced track coaches. Yet between them they won most of the important races in the middle 1970s.

John Walker was the son of a New Zealand cement contractor. The heavy construction work he did for his father built him into a solid, muscular man. At 6 feet, 1 inch, and 180 pounds, Walker seemed to carry too much weight to be a distance runner. His thick chest and heavy thighs made him seem more suitable for wrestling or for football.

But in spite of his size, Walker had always dreamed of being a runner.

With Peter Snell, a fellow New Zealander who won both the 800- and the 1,500-meter runs in the 1964 Olympics as his inspiration, Walker set his sights on the 1968 Olympics. In preparing for the Olympics, Walker had to fight through a great deal of pain to follow his rough training schedule. Sometimes his knees became so swollen that he could not straighten his legs. But pain rarely kept him from a hard workout or from winning a race.

Most times, the large, muscular Walker seemed out of place racing his swifter, lighter opponents. But he used his sheer strength and knowledge of racing strategy to win many grueling races.

As John Walker was struggling through painful workouts, Filbert Bayi of Tanzania was chasing gazelle and other animals through the fields near his home village of Karata. Bayi had never heard of a planned workout schedule such as Walker was running. Running was a joyous adventure for him. But sometimes he got more adventure than he bargained for. While most modern runners are bothered by an occasional dog, Bayi once found himself face to face with a leopard! But despite such hazards, Bayi enjoyed running.

At a wiry 5 feet, 9 inches tall, and 135 pounds, Filbert seemed to glide even more lightly over the ground than the great Kenyan runner, Keino. Bayi's style of running was even more outrageous than that of Keino's. Bayi actually sprinted out at the firing of the starting gun and often opened up a huge lead before his startled rivals realized what was happening.

Once in the lead, Bayi constantly broke a major rule of running: never look back. Filbert was always peeking behind to see where his opponents were. Sometimes he would let them gain ground on him, and then he would pull away into a big lead just before they caught up to him.

The personalities of Walker and Bayi were as opposite as their running styles. While the small, speedy front runner, Bayi, was quiet, calm, and almost shy, Walker, the strong and powerful fast finisher, was like a sailor on a three-day pass. He loved having loud and lively fun with his racing buddies.

The two men amazed each other when they first met. Bayi was simply overwhelmed when he heard what Walker ran in practices. He could not believe that any human could actually do that much hard running. Walker, in turn, was left speechless by

Bayi's burst from the starting line. Walker had been taught to run the mile at a relaxed, steady pace in the early part of the race. But when he tried that against Bayi, Bayi had built up such a lead by the halfway point that no one could catch him.

Most of the early encounters between Bayi and Walker were won by Bayi. Just two years after appearing on the world track scene in 1972, Filbert was already the best runner in the world. His 1974 time for a 1,500-meter race was 3:32.2, a new world record. (In that race, Walker had placed second at 3:32.5.)

When asked about his success, Bayi claimed he was still only learning how to race. He had received little coaching in Tanzania and had hoped to learn the secrets of mile racing from the other runners. But when Bayi ran a 3:56.4 mile on an indoor track in San Diego in 1975, most of his opponents wondered just *who* was doing the teaching. In winning that race, Bayi ended the string of 26 straight wins in middle-distance races previously set by Rick Wohlhuter, the United States' top middle-distance runner.

In May 1975, many of the world's top milers traveled to Jamaica for a special showdown. The mile entries included Bayi, Wohlhuter, top North

American miler Marty Liquori, Ireland's Eamonn Coghlan, a man with a deadly finishing sprint, but not Walker. Over 35,000 fans jammed the stadium.

Few runners expected a fast time that day because it was still too early in the season. Besides, the stadium was like a giant steam bath in the muggy Jamaican weather. But as the gun went off, no one was surprised to see Bayi zoom away from the starting line. His first quarter-mile time of under 57 seconds, though, was fast even for him. And by the halfway mark, Bayi had opened up a comfortable lead.

In spite of his quick start, Bayi seemed heavy-legged and not as bouncy and lively as usual. His rivals set out to catch him. First, it was Coghlan who gained ground, but Bayi responded with a spurt to keep his lead. Then Liquori charged furiously past Coghlan, closing in on Bayi in the last lap. But Bayi again burst away and won the race by 10 yards in a time of 3:51.0! Jim Ryun's eight-year-old mile record had finally been beaten!

Later that summer, on August 12, John Walker raced in the cooler climate of Sweden. Just as Bayi had run his finest race when Walker was absent, Walker was to run his finest race when Bayi was not there.

Filbert Bayi glides to a world record 3:51.0 mile in the steamy Jamaican heat. Marty Liquori (right) placed second, and the third- and fourth-place finishers also ran the mile in less than four minutes.

At the start of the contest, John ran his more traditional race, staying close to the shoulder of the leader for a half mile. During that time, there was no battling for position. In fact, none of the runners even attempted to pass another runner. This easy pace saved Walker from the wear and tear of battling other racers, and he was able to keep his mind on staying relaxed.

When John heard that his half-mile time was well under two minutes, he decided he had a chance for a very fast race. He bolted into the lead and pulled away from the pack at a swift, steady pace.

"Walker! Walker!" the crowd shouted as he battled through the last lap. His long, blond hair was streaming in the wind, and his arms and legs were pumping with all the strength he had. Walker reached the finish line in an incredible time of 3:49.4. That was more than a second and a half faster than the world record Bayi had set only three months earlier!

After Bayi and Walker's triumphs, most of the track experts looked forward to the 1,500-meter race at the 1976 Olympic Games in Montreal. With Bayi and Walker in the race, it promised to be one of the most exciting Olympic events of all time.

Powerful John Walker fights off fatigue as he drives himself to a world record 3:49.4 mile on August 12, 1975.

But the great match between the two world record holders never happened. Just before the Olympics started, the African nations left the Olympics in protest. They were upset that another Olympic nation—New Zealand—had allowed its soccer team to play in South Africa. They did not think Olympic teams should play in a country that separated white and black people by law.

Along with the other Tanzanian athletes, Bayi did not run in the Olympics. John Walker took the gold medal, but it was not a very satisfying victory. Without Bayi to force the pace, Walker's time was a slow 3:39.2—4:35 seconds less than the Olympic record for the 1,500-meter race.

After the disappointing Montreal meet, there was some hope that the two great runners could stay in top shape until the next Olympics in 1980. Then the world would at last see the great Olympic race they had missed in 1976. But politics as well as a host of new running stars pushed the two opposites into the background. Because of his country's boycott of the 1980 Moscow Games, Walker did not compete. Bayi did enter the games, but he was discouraged by two record-setting milers from Great Britain, Steve Ovett and Sebastian Coe. Filbert moved up to the 3,000-meter steeplechase where he

West Germany's Paul Heinz-Wellman seems to be the happiest, but it was the black-shirted Walker, coasting to a stop, who won this 1976 Olympic 1,500. Ivo Van Damme of Belgium (middle) placed second.

took second place to Poland's Bronislaw Malinowski.

The mile has seen many great races over the years. But track experts think that the "race that never happened" in Montreal in 1976 could have ranked with the best. The world may never get another chance to see an Olympic match between two such opposite world record holders.

On August 27, 1980, in Koblenz, West Germany, Steve Ovett sets a new world's record in the 1,500 meter at 3:31.4. West Germany's Thomas Wessinghage (right) came in second while Sebastian Coe, the co-record holder, missed the race.

7
Sebastian Coe & Steve Ovett

In 1979 track fans were just getting used to the idea that tall, powerful runners were taking over the middle-distance events. First, there had been John Walker, the mile record holder. And then there was Alberto Juantorena, a Cuban whose long strides had outlasted his rivals in both the 400- and the 800-meter races in the 1976 Olympic games. At 6 feet, 3 inches, and 185 pounds, Juantorena was so strong he was known in Cuba as "el Caballo" which means "the Horse."

So when 5-foot, 8-inch, 122-pound Sebastian Coe from Great Britain toed the starting line in Oslo, Norway, on July 5, 1979, hoping to break Juantorena's record for the 800-meter race, little was expected of him. But the track world was caught by surprise that day as Coe ran the two-lap, 800-meter race in 1:24.4. Sebastian's time was a full second better than the "unbeatable" Juantorena's world record!

Reporters rushed in to find out about this new star. But Coe did not have a lot of news to tell them. He was 22 years old and from Sheffield, England, and he had loved running ever since he could stand up. He had spent many hours running over the rugged countryside by his home, coached by his father, an engineer. Other than earning a degree in economics, he had just been quietly and scientifically training for world records.

One of the main reasons Coe had gone largely unnoticed was because of the success of Steve Ovett, a fellow Briton from Brighton. Ovett had begun to run at the age of 13 and had quickly made a name for himself as the top quarter-miler in his age group. Two years later, Steve came under the guidance of Coach Harry Wilsen. Wilsen, fortunately, had the wisdom to keep Ovett away from heavy training until the youngster had grown. He did not want his star pupil to burn out before he had reached his prime.

As Steve grew older, however, the training really increased. Once a month, he tackled Water Hole Hill and would charge up the steep chalk cliffs near Dover a total of six times during a workout.

Steve also mixed explosions of speed with distance running. Sixty-meter sprints were as important to his training as eight-mile runs.

Ovett was such an amazing runner with such a blend of speed and endurance that he could run with the best at almost any distance. His specialty —the 800 meter—happened to be the same event that Coe ran, but Ovett could also bury top distance runners. In September 1978, he challenged Kenya's great distance runner, Henry Rono, in a two-mile race. The two exchanged mid-race sprints to tire each other out. But in the end, Ovett still blazed a fast 220-yard finish to win. In the process, he set a world record with a time of 8:13.5.

But when Coe broke the 800-meter world record, he could no longer be ignored, and Ovett had to share the spotlight with his little-known country-man. When it was announced at the track that Coe would also run in the "Golden Mile" in Norway only 12 days later, many milers took notice. They figured that anyone who looked *that* strong at the end of a world record 800-meter race was capable of a good mile race, and they expected Coe to challenge John Walker's mile record.

The fact that few of the world's top milers had ever raced against Coe before made them all the more nervous. Everyone, including Coe himself, was eager to see what kind of a miler the new 800-meter record holder would make.

A tremendous group of milers had gathered for the Golden Dubai Mile. Eamonn Coghlan of Ireland, who had just broken the world indoor record for the mile at 3:52.6, was there along with two other record-breaking milers, Steve Scott from California and Steve Lacy, a graduate from the University of Wisconsin. (Indoor races are run on 220-yard or smaller tracks and outdoor races are usually run on 440-yard tracks. Separate records are kept, and indoor times are slower because runners have twice as many turns to go around while covering the same distance.) John Walker, the world record holder of the outdoor mile, also showed up to defend his title. David Moorcroft, John Robson, and John Williamson—all from Great Britain—and European champion, Thomas Wessinghage of West Germany, also joined the field. Steve Ovett was one of the few great milers who did not enter.

The Bislett Stadium in Oslo, Norway, was perfect for this great race. It was a fairly new track. The stands held over 15,000 fans and were close to the running surface. Athletes were often spurred on to make their best efforts by the screaming fans who seemed to be right on their shoulders. More than 30 world records had already been run on the Bislett track.

The contest in Oslo was only the third mile race in Coe's life, but he seemed even more relaxed than his veteran opponents. When the starting gun went off, Coe darted to the front of the pack. Because he was the smallest runner, he wanted to avoid the pushing and elbowing that happens at the start of a race as the runners fight for position.

As Coe reached the first turn, Steve Lacy dashed into the lead. Weakened by a recent illness, Lacy knew he could not run a good race. So he had decided to help others to a fast time by setting a quick, even pace. As Lacy sped around the track, the others followed, touring each of the first two quarters in 57 seconds. This meant an astounding half-mile time of 1:54! At this point, Lacy dropped out of the race, and Steve Scott took over. Scott ran the third lap so fast that only Coe could stay with him.

Just before the final lap, Coe swung out into the lead. Some thought that he might have moved too soon and that Scott would pass him at the end. But as Sebastian cruised around the artificial surface of the track, he gained more and more of

Sebastian Coe could just as well have been jogging for fun for all the strain he shows! But he is actually on his way to setting a world record in this 1979 Oslo race.

a lead. His smooth strides never shortened as he sped down the final stretch and hit the tape. Far down the track, John Walker knew that his record was gone.

Coe's time of 3:49.0 was a new world record. As in his 800-meter world record, it seemed as if Coe could have gone even faster. A month later, Sebastian ran a 1,500-meter race in 3:32.1 for his third world record that summer—a race only 1/10th of a second under Bayi's five-year-old record.

Once again the mile was back on top of the track world as the glamour race. The efforts by Sebastian Coe had helped bring the headlines back to that historic event. Coe had also triggered the most furious competition that the event has ever known. Steve Ovett, Eamonn Coghlan, John Walker, and others grimly set their sights on what had been unthinkable five years ago: a 3:45 mile.

In July 1980 at Oslo's Bislett Stadium, Steve Ovett edged past Coe's mile record with a 3:48.8 clocking. Two weeks later, also in Oslo, Ovett also tied Coe's 1,500 mark of 3:32.1. Now everyone was looking forward to the 1980 Moscow Olympics where Ovett and Coe would face each other in the 1,500 meter for the first time.

In their first Olympic contest, the 800-meter race, Coe let Ovett build up too big of a lead, and Ovett outsprinted the dawdling Coe to victory. It seemed as though Ovett was ready to end Sebastian's short reign as the king of the mile.

But the 1,500-meter event would soon decide who was really the better runner.

In the 1,500-meter race, Coe and Ovett easily glided through a slow first half. Then an East German runner, Jurgen Straub, shot into the lead and tried to run the two Englishmen into exhaustion before the final kick. Coe clung to the East German's shoulder with Ovett right behind. Around the final turn, Sebastian unleashed his sprint. Steve tried to match it, but Coe glided away from him and collapsed at the tape in first place with a time of 3:38.4, six seconds slower than the world record he shared with Ovett, who had finished third at 3:39.

Coe had broken Ovett's winning streak at 42 races and had stood up to the challenge of a great rival. But one month later on August 27, in a race that Coe missed because of back trouble, Ovett set still another 1,500-meter record with a time of 3:31.4. So the battle of the two champion milers continued, and the answer to the question of who was the better runner remained unanswered.

8
Mary
Decker

In 1974, 15-year-old Mary Decker was the top woman half-miler in the United States. Track experts thought she could become the first American woman in years to seriously challenge the Eastern Europeans in the distance events. If Mary was already this good, they figured, just wait until she grows up.

But as Mary grew, her legs began to throb. Even a short run would send jabs of pain through her legs for an entire day. And neither Mary nor her coaches could discover what was wrong. Before one race in 1976, she had to take a dozen aspirin to block out the pain in her legs. Mary managed to finish that race, and she even ended up as the winner, but the effect of the aspirin on her stomach was even worse than the pain in her legs.

After that grueling race, Decker decided she could not take any more pain. She gave up racing and hoped her body would somehow heal. But after a year of trying every cure that she could find, she was no better. It now seemed that Mary's short running career was over. The track star of the future was suddenly nothing but a memory in the track world.

Mary was born in Bunnvale, New Jersey, in 1958. Ever since she had been a young girl, Mary enjoyed being outdoors. But it was not until her family moved to California in 1968, when she was 11, that Mary began running.

In California Mary's racing career had begun out of sheer boredom! One day when she and a friend were trying to think of something to do, they heard about a cross-country race. Since neither girl even knew what cross-country was, they went to find out. When they discovered it was a distance race, Mary entered and won easily.

After that Mary decided to take running seriously, and she began training. Although she was only 5 feet tall and weighed less than 90 pounds, Mary could stay with most of the high school trackmen in their workouts. Running came so naturally to Mary that she broke three world records for women before her 14th birthday—the 880 yard (2:12.7) and the marathon (3 hours, 9 minutes), both for 12 year olds, and the mile record for 13 year olds (4:55).

Suddenly the young pony-tailed speedster became one of the United States' most popular track stars. Track officials wanted her at their meets to help draw spectators. Decker had become so famous that even stories about her habit of eating plain spaghetti before every race made the news.

In 1974 the tiny 14 year old was sent with the United States track team to run in the Soviet Union. It was at this meet that Decker first showed her fierce competitive nature as well as her inexperience. Mary was running in a relay race, just ahead of a much larger Soviet runner. The race was very close, and the Soviet woman bumped Mary from behind. Shortly after that she bumped Mary even harder, throwing her off-stride. Mary was furious and suddenly threw her baton at the other runner!

The spectators gasped. No one had ever seen such a fit of anger in a major track meet. By throwing her baton, Mary automatically disqualified her team in the race. The Soviet woman was also disqualified for interfering. It was one of the few races ever in world competition where there was no winner!

Tiny Mary Decker exclaims for joy after setting a women's world indoor record for the 880-yard run in 1974 with a time of 2:07.3. For the next five years of her career, however, Mary found little to cheer about.

In spite of her temper and inexperience, by the end of 1974, Mary proved to be the top woman half-miler in the United States. But after that, nothing seemed to go right for her. Several track stars, including America's top distance runner, Steve Prefontaine, warned her to start taking it easy. They were shocked at what Mary's coach expected of her. But Mary, unfortunately, continued to follow her coach's orders and met with disaster.

One day she ran in a marathon, and the very next day she raced in two more events. By the end of that week, Mary was in the hospital.

Mary finally switched coaches. During this time, her grandmother also died and her parents got a divorce. All of these changes in Mary's life began to affect her running. In one race during this difficult period, Mary cried all the way through the race and finished far behind the other runners.

Then the terrible leg pains came. Mary tried everything the doctors suggested. But even running in special shoes and putting her legs in casts for weeks were worthless cures.

Fortunately, a top distance runner from New Zealand heard of Mary's troubles. Dick Quax, a world record holder at 5,000 meters, once had had the same thing happen to him. According to Quax, the muscles of Mary's legs were simply growing too large for the sheaths that surrounded them. He told Mary an operation could open the sheaths up enough to relieve the pressure that was causing the pain.

Mary agreed to try the operation in late 1977. At first her legs felt worse than ever. But in a few months the pain was gone, and Mary was at last back on the road to fame. Under the careful guidance of Dick Quax, Mary trained more carefully than ever before.

In January of 1980, the beginning of the track season, a healthy Mary Decker was in Auckland, New Zealand, ready to show the world what she could do. As Decker blazed around the track, it was obvious that she was in top form. Her time of 4:21.7 set a new world outdoor mile record for women, breaking the record 4:22.1 time set by Natalia Maracesce of Rumania in 1979.

The next month, Mary was in New York City at an indoor meet, ready to try for another record—the 1,500 meter. When Mary ran the first quarter of the race in just over 60 seconds, the men milers nearly choked. Decker was running faster than Eamonn Coghlan had run when he had broken the world indoor record for men! Appearing strong and relaxed, Decker blazed around the track with such confidence and bounce that she actually seemed to be enjoying herself! Her final time for the 1,500 meters was 4:00.8, a new women's world indoor record.

One week later at the Houston Astrodome in Texas, Mary set out after the indoor mile record. Determined to run a more even pace than she had in New York, she glided easily into the lead. But

Decker's smooth stride carries her toward the finish line and an indoor world mile record of 4:17.55 on February 16, 1980, in Houston, Texas.

by the quarter mile, Mary was already running all by herself in a time of 60.8 seconds. She could hardly believe it and felt as fresh as if she were just trotting.

The crowd screamed their encouragement as Mary sped around the track. Still feeling strong at the finish, she posted a 4:17.55 mile time. Decker's mile was the fastest woman's mile ever run and 11 seconds faster than Francie Larrieu's 4:28.5 United States' indoor record set five years earlier.

Mary had already broken two world records in one month, but she was still not through. At the San Diego Invitational track meet on February 22, Mary became the first woman to break 2 minutes for 880 yards. Mary's time of 1:59.7 was a new world record. It was also her fourth world record for the year and her third indoor world record for the month!

July 1980 proved to be another incredible record-setting month for Decker. In Stuttgart, West Germany, Mary set an American record for the 1,500 meter. Her time of 4:01.17 was 1.53 seconds faster than the previous record set by Jan Merrill.

Only three days after her 1,500-meter run, Mary broke another American record held by Jan Merrill. On July 15 at the Bislett Games in Oslo, Norway, Mary ran her first 3,000-meter race and set a new record of 8:38.73. Mary's time was almost 4 seconds better than the old record.

And then on July 17, five days after she had set the new American record for the 1,500 meter, Mary broke her own record. At a meet in Philadelphia, Decker crossed the finish line in a time of 4:00.87. This was another record for Decker, her third one for July and, incredibly enough, her seventh one for the year!

Track officials had to look far down the track to spot the second-place runner in this 880-yard race in San Diego. But even with no competition to challenge her, Mary ran her third world record in one month.

Mary not only continues to be one of the world's top woman track stars, she is also one of the most friendly people in the track world. Mary always tries to get to know all of her fellow runners, male or female. She does not have the quiet, serious dedication to victory like that of some of her rivals. "What's the fun of racing if we can't be friends?" asks Mary.

Milers talk seriously of Mary's chances of becoming the first woman to run a four-minute mile. Until she came along, no one even considered the possibility of any woman running that fast. Now wherever Mary goes, the crowds seem eager to cheer her on to such a record. (To date the fastest woman runner is Tatyana Kazankina of the U.S.S.R. who in 1976 ran the 1,500-meter race in 3:56.0, the equivalent of running a 4:14.9 mile.)

Mary says she can hear the crowds, especially when she is running by herself in a race. And since she is usually at the head of the pack, racing no one but herself, she must be hearing the cheers very well these days!